Jenny Archer, Author

by Ellen Conford

Illustrated by Diane Palmisciano

Little, Brown and Company
Boston   Toronto   London

Text copyright © 1989 by Conford Enterprises Ltd.
Illustrations copyright © 1989 by Diane Palmisciano

First Edition

Springboard and design is a trademark of
Little, Brown and Company (Inc.)

Library of Congress Cataloging-in-Publication Data

Conford, Ellen.
  Jenny Archer, author / by Ellen Conford;
illustrated by Diane Palmisciano. —1st ed.
      p.   cm. — (A Springboard book)
  Summary: Stymied by an assignment to write her autobiography, Jenny decides to enhance her life story by using her con-
siderable imagination.
  ISBN 0-316-15255-2
  [1. Imagination — Fiction.   2. Schools — Fiction.
3. Humorous stories.]   I. Palmisciano, Diane, ill.   II. Title.
PZ7.C7593Je 1989   88-30792
[Fic] — dc19   CIP
                                                         AC

10 9 8 7 6 5 4 3 2

WOR

*Published simultaneously in Canada
by Little, Brown & Company (Canada) Limited*

Printed in the United States of America

Jenny Archer,
Author

1

Jenny Archer felt very proud.

She stood in front of her class. She looked at the A+ and the gold star on her composition.

Her teacher, Mrs. Pike, said, "Now, boys and girls, let's open our ears and listen carefully. Jenny is going to read her composition."

Jenny's friend Beth clapped her hands silently.

Jenny pushed her glasses back on her nose and cleared her throat.

" 'My Favorite Place. My favorite place is my own room,' " she read. " 'I keep all my favorite things there, like my dinosaur models and my books and my stamp collection and my goldfish, Phyllis.

" 'When I am alone, I can pretend that the dinosaurs are alive. When I look at my stamps, I can pretend that I'm living in another country. When I read a book, I can become part of the story and have an exciting adventure.

" 'The kitchen is just for cooking. The dining room is just for eating.

" 'But my room is just for me.' "

Jenny looked up from her paper. Beth flashed her a thumbs-up sign. Some of the other kids looked bored. But Mrs. Pike had a big smile on her face.

"Bravo, Jenny! You said a lot in just a few words."

Clifford Stern raised his hand. He didn't wait for Mrs. Pike to call on him. "I thought you wanted us to use a lot of words. I didn't know we were supposed to write a *short* composition."

"It's not how long or short a paper is," said Mrs. Pike. "What counts is how well you write it. Jenny writes very well. She might even become an author some day."

Beth made clapping motions again.

Jenny beamed as she walked back to her seat.

An author!

Jenny had never thought about being an author. She never thought much about writing at all, except when she had to do it for school.

All along, she'd been a talented writer and didn't even know it!

She could hardly wait to tell her parents she was going to be an author.

"I think you'll enjoy your next creative writing project," Mrs. Pike said. "I want each of you to write an autobiography —"

Clifford Stern raised his hand. "What's an autobiography?"

"If you'll stop interrupting, Clifford, you'll find out. An autobiography is the story of your own life. I want each of you to write the story of your life."

"Does it have to be long?" Clifford didn't even bother to raise his hand this time.

"Remember what I said," Mrs. Pike went on. "It's not how long the story is, it's how well you tell it. Everybody has his or her own special story to tell. Everybody's life is different. Don't you think it will be exciting to read all those stories?"

Some of the kids mumbled, "Yes." Others still looked bored.

Jenny tapped her pencil against her teeth.

The story of her life? She was only a kid. She didn't have a story to tell yet.

She'd hardly even had a life yet.

2

"I'm going to be an author," Jenny said. Her mother looked up from the potato she was peeling. Her father looked up from the salad he was tossing.

"Really?" he said. "And when did you decide this?"

"In school today. Mrs. Pike said that I might be an author some day. She said so in front of the whole class."

"That's wonderful," said Mrs. Archer. "I

used to write poetry when I was younger. I loved to write."

"I don't know if I love to write." Jenny folded three paper napkins and put them on the table.

"We have to write our autbog — our autobog — I mean, our life story," she said.

"Autobiography," said Mr. Archer. "I had to do that when I was in school."

"We did, too," said Mrs. Archer.

"What did you write?" Jenny asked.

"I don't remember."

Mr. Archer smiled. "I wrote a lot about our family. About Grandma and Grandpa and their parents. It was a long time ago."

Jenny pulled off her glasses and wiped the lenses with the bottom of her Godzilla T-shirt. "But I don't have a story. Nothing interesting has ever happened to me in my whole life."

"That's not so," her father said. "There was the time you tried to sell our house so you could buy Mom a birthday present."

"Hmm," said Jenny.

"There was the time you caught burglars robbing Beth's house," said her mother.

"You're right," said Jenny. "That's pretty interesting. But, except for that, absolutely nothing interesting has ever happened to me."

"But you have such a good imagination," her mother said.

Her father grinned. "Sometimes your imagination is *too* good."

"You can make your autobiography interesting," her mother went on, "if you write it in an interesting way."

Jenny put her glasses back on. "That's what Mrs. Pike said."

"See?" Mrs. Archer put the potato in a pot. "And Mrs. Pike said you write well. I'll bet you can write a terrific autobiography."

Jenny sighed. "I'll try," she said. "But I wish I had a more exciting life to write about."

3

"Chapter One," Jenny wrote. "I Am Born." She tapped her pencil against her teeth. She twisted a strand of her hair around a finger.

She couldn't remember a thing about being born.

She walked downstairs. Her big black dog, Barkley, followed her. His tail wagged happily.

"We can't go out now, Barkley. I'm writing a book."

Jenny's mother was in the living room doing a crossword puzzle.

"Mom," Jenny began, "did anything exciting happen when I was born?"

Mrs. Archer laughed. "It was the most exciting thing that ever happened to me."

"But everyone gets born," said Jenny. "Was there anything different or unusual about me?"

"You were beautiful," said her mother. "Perfectly normal and healthy."

Jenny sighed. "That's so boring."

"Believe me, Jenny," her mother said. "It wasn't boring."

Jenny started back upstairs to her room. Barkley ran to the front door and back to the stairs. He wagged his tail. He wagged his whole body.

"Okay, Barkley," said Jenny. "I think I'm

better with dogs than I am with stories."

Barkley was a very good dog. Jenny had trained him. He never tugged at the leash or tried to run away.

She walked down the front steps. Barkley was right at her heels.

"Let's go to Wilson's house," said Jenny. Wilson Wynn was a good friend of Jenny's. He lived two blocks away.

Jenny rang the doorbell. Barkley wagged his tail. He liked Wilson, even though Wilson didn't like dogs.

Wilson opened the front door. Barkley tried to lick his bare foot.

Wilson squeezed his eyes shut and stood as still as a stone.

"No, Barkley!" said Jenny. "Sit."

Barkley sat at her feet.

Jenny could hear the television in the living room.

"Do you want to go for a walk with us?" Jenny asked.

Wilson opened his eyes and looked at Barkley.

"I don't think so," he said. "I'm watching a really exciting movie."

"What's it about?"

"There's this little baby," Wilson said, "and she has scarlet fever."

"What's scarlet fever?" Jenny asked.

"It's a very bad disease. And they don't know if the baby will live or die. And they're waiting for the doctor to come. But there's a blizzard and he can't get up the mountain."

"Wow!" said Jenny. "That really does sound exciting."

Suddenly her eyes opened wide. "Wilson, I'm so glad I came to see you!"

"So am I," said Wilson. "But if you want to watch the show with me, would you leave Barkley outside?"

"I can't watch it now." Jenny was already halfway down the walk. "I have to write a book."

4

"Chapter One," Jenny wrote. "I Am Born. I was born on a dark and stormy night in a hut near the Amazon River. The doctor tried to get to my mother, but the hurricane was so bad he couldn't steer his boat.

"As soon as I was born, I got jungle fever. I was also very small. For weeks my parents didn't know if I would live or die. The doctor said it was a miracle that I didn't die from the jungle fever and my very smallness."

Jenny read what she had written. She smiled.

"Excellent," she told herself.

But it was only five lines. Five lines seemed pretty short for a chapter.

Jenny remembered what Mrs. Pike had said. "It doesn't matter if it's long or short. What counts is how well you tell it."

Jenny thought she had told Chapter One very well.

She took another piece of paper and wrote, "Chapter Two."

But she couldn't think of a thing to write in Chapter Two. Chapter One was so exciting that it was hard for Jenny to think up something better.

"Jenny!" her mother called. "Come on. We're going to see Grandma and Grandpa Archer."

"Oh, good," Jenny said. "Maybe they can give me some ideas for my story."

Jenny's father had said he'd written about his parents and grandparents. Maybe Jenny had some famous relatives that she didn't know about.

Grandma and Grandpa Archer lived about a half hour away from Jenny's house. They had an apartment in a three-story building named Boxwood Gardens. Even though the building had only three floors, there was an elevator.

Jenny was usually so eager to see her grandparents that she would run up the stairs. Her father and mother waited for the elevator. Jenny always beat them to the third floor.

But today she was thinking so hard about her life story that she stood quietly until the elevator came.

Grandma and Grandpa Archer hugged and kissed Jenny. Then they hugged and kissed Jenny's mother and father.

"Is the elevator working today?" asked Grandma.

"Yes," said Jenny's mother. "Was it broken?"

"We had a lot of trouble with it this week," said Grandpa. "It kept getting stuck between floors."

"I was trapped between the second and third floors for half an hour yesterday," Grandma said.

"Trapped?" Jenny's eyes grew big and round.

"It was her big adventure for the week," Grandpa joked.

Grandma laughed. "It wasn't exactly like getting stuck in the Empire State Building. But it wasn't a lot of fun, either."

Trapped, Jenny thought. In the Empire State Building . . .

While they had milk and coffee and cake, Jenny's mother told her grandparents about her A+ composition.

"That's wonderful," said Grandma.

"You always did have a good imagination," Grandpa said. He cut Jenny another slice of cake.

"Now we have to write our life story," said Jenny. "Did we have any famous people in our family?"

"My father was a tailor," said Grandpa.

"Was he famous?" Jenny asked eagerly.

"No, but he was a very good tailor."

Jenny sighed.

Grandpa looked at Jenny's father and winked. "But my mother was an opera singer," he said. "And my grandmother robbed stage coaches from Kansas to Arizona."

"Wow!" Jenny nearly knocked over her milk glass. "Like in the movies?"

Grandpa nodded.

"Stop that, Herb!" scolded Grandma. "He's just teasing, Jenny."

"Oh." Jenny couldn't hide her disappointment.

Her father ruffled her hair. "I'm sorry we

haven't got a more exciting family tree."

"So am I," said Jenny sadly. "I'll bet nobody else in the class would have a great-great-grandmother who —"

Jenny stopped in the middle of her sentence.

Maybe she didn't have an exciting family tree. But maybe she didn't really need one.

She had something better.

She had a good imagination.

5

"Chapter Two," Jenny wrote. "My Famous Family."

She closed her eyes. In her mind she could picture her great-great-grandmother. She was mounted on a big white horse and waving a rifle at a stagecoach.

"I come from a long line of famous people," Jenny wrote. "My great-great-grandmother was named . . ."

Jenny twisted her hair. Buffalo Belle! she thought.

". . . Buffalo Belle Archer. She was a notorious stagecoach robber. She and her gang held up stagecoaches from Kansas to Arizona.

"But one day she was captured. She went to jail. While she was in jail she took up singing to pass the time."

This is great! Jenny thought. She remembered what Grandpa said about his mother being an opera star. He was only teasing, but it was a great idea.

"When Buffalo Belle Archer got out of jail," Jenny wrote, "she was such a good singer that she became an opera star. Soon, she was famous all over the world.

"She was no longer a gunslinger. Now she was a gun*singer*."

Jenny grinned. A little humor was always good.

Grandpa Archer's father had been a tailor. Jenny pushed her glasses back on her nose. Being a tailor wasn't exciting at all. Maybe she should make him a sailor.

Her eyes lit up. She grabbed her pencil. She began to write as fast as she could. "My great-grandfather was a sailor. He was the first person to sail around the world in a rowboat.

"But first he was a pirate. They called him . . . Blackbeard Archer, the Devil of the Seven Seas."

My, thought Jenny, I *do* have a good imagination.

She was still writing about Blackbeard Archer when her friend Beth Moore ran into her room. Jenny was so lost in her writing that she hadn't even heard the doorbell ring.

"Guess what?" Beth said. She reached down to scratch Barkley's ears. "We're going to the circus tomorrow."

"Lucky you," said Jenny. "I didn't even know the circus was in town."

"It's not a big famous circus," said Beth. "It's called the Amazing Attractions Circus. They're at the Civic Center today and Sunday."

Jenny put her pencil down. "I wish I could go. Maybe my parents will take me."

"They don't have to!" Beth looked as if she would burst with her good news. "My mother got four tickets! You can go with us!"

"Wow!" Jenny jumped up from her chair. She hugged Beth. Beth hugged her. Barkley jumped between them wanting to be hugged, too.

Jenny forgot about her autobiography. She forgot about Blackbeard Archer. She forgot about becoming an author.

All she could think of was lion tamers, and clowns, and cotton candy.

6

Mr. and Mrs. Moore had bought front-row tickets for the circus. Jenny and Beth could hardly believe they were sitting so close to the performers.

Jenny had been to the Coleman's Colossal Circus once. It was enormous. There were three rings and everything seemed to happen at the same time.

It was hard to watch three acts at once. Jenny thought this smaller circus was more fun.

There were clowns and acrobats and beautiful trick horseback riders. But only one act went on at a time.

A lion tamer with a big black mustache and long hair entered the ring.

Jenny gasped as the man stepped into a cage with three lions inside. He twirled his whip over his head. The lions started trotting around their cage in a circle.

The lions roared. They jumped over each other and then jumped over the lion tamer. Finally, each of the lions leaped through a flaming hoop.

Jenny had to peek between her fingers to watch the last part. She was afraid that one of the lions would get burned.

Jenny and Beth thought the clowns were wonderful. One clown ran after another with a bucket of water and dumped it on him. Then the wet clown grabbed a bucket and began chasing the first clown.

They raced around the ring. They stopped

right in front of Jenny and Beth. The second clown raised the bucket.

The girls squealed and covered their heads. But instead of water, a shower of confetti hit them.

Everybody laughed. One of the clowns reached into his pocket and pulled out a giant lollipop. He bowed deeply and handed it to Jenny. The audience clapped and cheered.

The clown patted Jenny and Beth on their heads. Then he picked up the bucket and started running after the other clowns.

Jenny stared at the huge lollipop and the confetti all over her skirt. She had practically been part of the circus. She had almost been an assistant clown.

"Isn't this great?" Beth said.

Jenny leaned over so she could talk to Beth's parents.

"This is the best circus I have ever seen," she said. "I'm going to put it in my auto-biography."

7

The next morning Jenny woke up with a sore throat. Her father felt her forehead. He said that she didn't seem to have a fever.

"But you'd better stay home today," her mother said. "I'll call Mrs. Butterfield."

Mrs. Butterfield was Jenny's baby-sitter. Jenny told her parents over and over again that she didn't need a baby-sitter. She was no baby.

So her father started calling Mrs. Butterfield her person-sitter.

Mrs. Butterfield came right over and Jenny's parents went off to work.

Even though Jenny felt too old to have a baby-sitter, she liked Mrs. Butterfield. Mrs. Butterfield liked television. When she stayed with Jenny they watched TV together.

In the afternoon, Mrs. Butterfield's favorite soap operas were on.

"I never miss them," she told Jenny.

Jenny's throat didn't hurt so much after lunch, but she started sniffling and sneezing.

"I think you're just getting a cold." Mrs. Butterfield looked at her watch. "Time for my soaps," she said.

She turned on the TV. She sat down on the couch next to Jenny. Barkley flopped down on the floor between the couch and the television set.

Mrs. Butterfield covered Jenny's legs with a wool blanket and gave her a box of tissues.

It turned out that Mrs. Butterfield needed the tissues more than Jenny. On the first show, her favorite character was badly hurt in a train wreck. At the end, Mrs. Butterfield didn't know whether he would recover.

"This is great!" Jenny said. "I wish I could watch this all the time."

The next program was even better. It was about a woman who had a twin sister. But she didn't know she had a twin sister. They were separated at birth.

Now, twenty-five years later, the evil twin planned to kill the good twin and take over her life.

"Wow!" said Jenny. "Maybe I have a twin sister somewhere that I don't know about."

"You wouldn't want a sister like that," Mrs. Butterfield said.

"I guess not," Jenny agreed. "But even if I did, why would she want to be me? My life isn't —"

Jenny stopped. She pushed her glasses back on her nose. Her eyes moved away from the television screen.

Why can't I have an evil twin sister? she asked herself. It's *my* autobiography. I'm writing it. An evil twin sister would definitely make my life more interesting.

I think I'll name her Hortense.

8

"Chapter Three," Jenny wrote that night. "My Evil Twin."

Jenny sat for a moment or two, staring at the chapter title. She got up and stretched her arms. She walked around her room. She sprinkled food into the fish bowl. Phyllis bobbed up to nibble at it.

Jenny couldn't decide what her secret evil twin sister should try to do to her.

Maybe I ought to watch more soap operas, she thought.

The telephone rang. Jenny ignored it. She began to pace around the room in the other direction.

"Jenny!" Her mother called. "It's Grandma Archer. I told her you stayed home today. She wants to say hi."

In a flash, Jenny remembered. Elevator! Empire State Building.

She ran to the phone in her parents' bedroom.

"Grandma!" she shouted. "I'm writing my autobiography. You gave me a great idea!"

"I'm glad," said Grandma. "But I don't know why you need ideas about your own life story."

"You gave me an idea to make it more interesting," Jenny explained.

While she was talking to her grandmother, Jenny heard the doorbell. Barkley started woofing.

Jenny was just saying good-bye to Grandma Archer when Beth walked into her room.

"Are you sick?" asked Beth.

"Just a cold," Jenny said. "Don't get too close to me. I'm probably catching."

"I'm glad it wasn't the circus that made you sick," Beth said. "I thought maybe you ate too much and got a stomachache."

"Did you start writing your autobiography yet?" Jenny asked.

"I finished it."

"You finished it already?" Jenny repeated. "I'm only on Chapter Three of mine."

"You have *chapters*?" Beth looked impressed. "Your life must be a lot more exciting than mine."

"Do you want to read what I've got so far?" Jenny hoped Beth would say yes. She was eager to show her writing to someone.

"Sure," said Beth.

Jenny handed her the first two chapters. Beth's eyes grew wide as she read about the jungle hut and Buffalo Belle.

"Wow!" Beth handed the pages back to

Jenny. "What a great family. All I wrote was that we moved a lot."

"I'm just getting started," said Jenny. "Wait till I finish Chapter Three."

"You'd better hurry up and finish," said Beth. "Mrs. Pike said we have to hand them in by Friday."

"No problem," said Jenny. "I think I really have a talent for writing."

9

"Chapter Three," Jenny wrote again. "Horrible Hortense."

She smiled. She loved the way it sounded.

"I never knew I had an evil twin sister until last summer. I was visiting the Empire State Building in New York City. I took the elevator up.

"There was only one other person in the elevator.

"*She looked exactly like me.*"

Jenny shivered a little. She could see her evil twin clearly in her mind. She could see the elevator stop between the 99th and the 100th floor.

" 'I have been on your trail for years,' the stranger said. 'If you think I'm going to let you inherit the family fortune, you're mistaken.' "

Good, Jenny thought. Good. She wrote faster and faster. It was hard for her pencil to keep up with her imagination.

Before she knew it she was on Chapter Seven, "How My Father Gambled Away Our Family Fortune."

Just three more chapters and her life story would be done. Jenny had decided that her autobiography ought to have ten chapters because she was ten years old.

She would definitely have her story done by Friday, even with copying it over.

Jenny went back to school on Wednesday. As she walked home with Wilson and Beth, she could hardly think of anything except her autobiography.

She was going to write the last two chapters this afternoon, and copy it over tonight. She couldn't wait to give it to Mrs. Pike. She was sure her teacher would ask her to read it out loud.

"My mother wishes you'd come over and play with Tyler," Wilson said. Tyler was Wilson's baby brother. He was getting new teeth. He cried a lot. But he liked Jenny to hold him. Sometimes he stopped crying when she did.

"I'd better not," Jenny said. "I don't want to give Tyler my cold."

"Why don't we go over to my house?" said Beth. "I have a new Bugs Bunny video."

Jenny loved Bugs Bunny cartoons. But she shook her head. She could watch the video another time. She had to think of her writing first.

Jenny worked all afternoon and an hour after dinner. She finally finished her autobiography. She copied it over neatly. She was about to show it to her parents when she thought, maybe I'll wait. They were so pleased with the good mark on her last paper. She would let them see her autobiography after Mrs. Pike gave her an A+ and the gold star.

Jenny was sure they'd be very proud of her.

10

Thursday morning Jenny gave her autobiography to Mrs. Pike. She had even made a cover for it, just like a real book. She had drawn a picture of Buffalo Belle on a big white horse.

"You're a day early, Jenny," said Mrs. Pike. "Good for you."

"I'll bet she asks you to read it out loud," Beth said.

"I wouldn't be surprised," said Jenny. "I must say I think it's very interesting."

When Jenny came back to the room after lunch, her story was on Mrs. Pike's desk. She was looking at it, and frowning.

When she saw Jenny, she frowned some more.

"She looks angry," Beth said.

"Do you think she could be angry about my autobiography?" Jenny asked. "She's looking at it."

"Don't be silly," Beth said. "Why should she be angry about it?"

"I don't know," said Jenny. "But I have a funny feeling."

All afternoon Jenny worried about Mrs. Pike and her story. What could be wrong? Buffalo Belle, Blackbeard Archer, Daredevil Dan, the lion tamer . . . How her father lost the family fortune in a poker game . . . It was a wonderful story. Jenny was sure no one else in the class would have an autobiography like hers.

When the bell rang at three o'clock, Mrs. Pike dismissed the class.

"Stay here, Jenny," she said. She was frowning again.

"Uh oh," Jenny whispered. "Wait for me outside, Beth."

Beth nodded and scooted out of the room.

Jenny walked up to Mrs. Pike's desk. There was an envelope on it. It was addressed to Mr. and Mrs. Archer.

"Are you sending a note to my parents?"

"Yes, I am," said Mrs. Pike. "Have them sign the note and return it to me tomorrow."

"But what did I do?" Jenny asked. "Is it about my autobiography?"

"It certainly is," said Mrs. Pike. "I'm very disappointed in you, Jenny."

Jenny felt terrible. She looked down at the floor. She had imagined Mrs. Pike's smile when she called Jenny to the front of the room to read her story. She had imagined the whole class applauding when she finished.

She had never imagined Mrs. Pike being disappointed.

"This isn't your autobiography," said Mrs. Pike.

"But it is," Jenny said. "I wrote it myself."

Maybe Mrs. Pike thought she had copied it from a book. It was a very good story. Jenny was sure of that. Maybe Mrs. Pike didn't think Jenny was talented enough to write such a good autobiography.

"Daredevil Dan Green, the lion tamer?" said Mrs. Pike. "Your evil twin sister, Hortense? Was she born in the middle of that hurricane, too?"

"Oops," said Jenny. "I forgot about that. But I can fix it."

"Don't change a word," said Mrs. Pike coldly. "I want your parents to read it just the way it is."

"What's the matter with it?" Jenny asked. "What did I do wrong?"

"It's all *lies*," said Mrs. Pike. "Did you really expect me to believe this?"

"But you said —"

"Give this to your parents," Mrs. Pike said. She handed Jenny the note. "Bring me an answer tomorrow." She turned her back on Jenny and started erasing the chalkboard.

Jenny shoved the note in her pocket and ran out of the room.

Beth and Wilson were waiting for her on the school steps.

"What did she want?" asked Beth. "Was it about your autobiography?"

Jenny nodded. She thought she might cry if she tried to talk.

Wilson could see how bad Jenny felt. He thought Jenny wasn't afraid of anything. She hardly ever cried. He was worried. He patted her gently on the shoulder.

"Well, if she didn't like your autobiography," said Beth, nervously, "she's going to hate mine. It's so boring."

Jenny didn't understand what was going on.

Mrs. Pike had made her feel as horrible as Horrible Hortense.

But what had Jenny done that was so horrible?

11

Jenny's mother usually got home from work at three-thirty. Jenny started waiting for her in front of the house at three-fifteen. Mrs. Archer drove into the garage at twenty to four. Jenny felt as if she had been waiting for hours.

Mrs. Archer gave Jenny a kiss and a hug. Jenny gave Mrs. Archer the note.

"What's this?"

"It's a note from my teacher. About my autobiography. I don't think she liked it."

Mrs. Archer tore open the envelope. She read the note silently. "You're right," she told Jenny. "She didn't like it."

"But why?" asked Jenny. "She didn't tell me."

"Let me read it," said Mrs. Archer.

She sat down at the table with Jenny's life story. Jenny sat down at the chair next to her mother and waited.

"You're making me nervous," said Mrs. Archer. "I can't read when you're staring at me like that."

Jenny turned her chair around. "I won't watch," she said. "What part are you up to?"

"Horrible Hortense," said Mrs. Archer. She sounded as if she was trying not to laugh.

"Is it funny?" Jenny asked. "I wasn't trying to make it funny. Except for Buffalo Belle, the gunsinger."

"Shh," said Mrs. Archer.

Jenny kept twisting around in her chair to see if her mother had finished.

Finally Mrs. Archer said, "You can look now."

Jenny turned around. Her mother was smiling broadly.

"It's wonderful," she said. "I love it. You have a great imagination. Of course, I always knew that."

"Then, what's wrong?" asked Jenny. "Why is Mrs. Pike mad at me?"

"It's a misunderstanding," said Mrs. Archer. "Mrs. Pike wanted you to write your autobiography. You made up a story."

"But that's what an autobiography is," said Jenny. "A life *story*."

Mrs. Archer shook her head. "That's the part you didn't understand. Mrs. Pike thought you were lying on purpose. You wrote a good story, but it's not true."

"But she didn't say it had to be true! This is much more interesting than real life."

"I'll write her a note to explain. Why don't you write your real autobiography? You can hand it in tomorrow. I'm sure Mrs. Pike won't stay angry at you."

Jenny hoped not. Up until now, she'd thought Mrs. Pike liked her.

When her father got home, he read Jenny's story. He laughed a lot while he was reading it.

"It's not supposed to be funny," Jenny said.

"It's fun to read," he explained. "Where did you get all these ideas?"

"From Grandma and Grandpa and Mrs. Butterfield's soap operas. And Wilson," Jenny said. "Plus I have a great imagination."

"You certainly do," her father agreed.

Jenny wrote her real autobiography after dinner. It was only two pages long.

She sighed.

What good is an imagination, she wondered, if you don't get to use it?

12

The next morning Jenny gave Mrs. Pike her mother's note.

"I didn't know we were supposed to write about our *real* life," she said.

She pulled her true story out from her notebook. She put it on Mrs. Pike's desk. "I'm sorry you didn't like the other one," she said. "I thought it was much better than the truth."

Jenny sat down and watched Mrs. Pike open the envelope. She watched Mrs. Pike's face as she read Mrs. Archer's note.

Mrs. Pike started to smile. She looked up from the page and smiled right at Jenny. Jenny could see that she wasn't angry anymore.

That must be a really good note, Jenny thought. Maybe her mother had writing talent, too.

Mrs. Pike called Jenny to her desk. "I'm sorry I was so angry yesterday. Perhaps I didn't explain clearly enough that an autobiography must be the truth."

"Maybe I didn't hear it clearly," Jenny said. "I guess I won't be a writer after all. Maybe I'll be a clown."

"But you're a good writer," said Mrs. Pike. "You have a very lively imagination."

"I know," said Jenny. "But it just gets me in trouble."

Mrs. Pike collected the rest of the autobiographies from the class.

"I'll bet she asks you to read yours out loud," Beth said.

"I'll bet she doesn't," said Jenny. "But I don't care. I'm going to be a clown."

After lunch, as soon as everyone had sat down, Mrs. Pike picked up a bunch of papers from her desk.

"I've read some of your autobiographies this morning. I want you to hear one I really enjoyed. Jenny, come up here please."

Beth squeezed her arm. "*See?* I told you."

Jenny couldn't believe it. Why would Mrs. Pike want her to read her very boring true life story? Jenny thought she was just trying to be nice. She was probably trying to make up for yesterday.

"Jenny wrote two autobiographies," Mrs. Pike said. "One was her real life story. But she made up the other one from her own imagination."

Jenny hoped the class wouldn't be too bored when she read her real story.

Clifford Stern crossed his eyes.

Mrs. Pike handed Jenny her paper.

Buffalo Belle was on the cover.

"You want me to read *this* one?" Jenny asked.

Mrs. Pike nodded. "Jenny made up a very interesting life story for herself. Let's open our ears and listen carefully."

Jenny folded the cover back. At the top of the first page she saw an A+ and a gold star. Next to the star Mrs. Pike had written: "Extra credit for an exciting story!"

Jenny was so proud she felt as if she were glowing.

She looked out at her classmates. Beth was making clapping motions with her hands. Clifford Stern was trying to touch his nose with the tip of his tongue.

" 'Chapter One,' " Jenny began. " 'I Am Born.' "